PHINEAS L. MACGUIRE . . .

GETS COOKING!

For Win Hill and Gavin Schulz,
two of my favorite geniuses

The author would like to thank the most fabulous Caitlyn Dlouhy and the
most marvelous Ariel Colletti for being utterly fabulous and marvelous,
and she wants to give a big tip of the hat to Lyn Streck, science teacher
extraordinaire. Thanks to Kaitlin Severini, pretty much the best copy
editor ever, and to Sonia Chaghatzbanian, the most marvelous book
designer. Thank you to the fantastic Laura Ferguson for all of her fantastic
work, and lots of love and gratitude to the usual gang of family and
friends who keep the author centered and sane, which is no easy job.

Also by Frances O'Roark Dowell

*Chicken Boy • Dovey Coe • Falling In • The Kind of Friends We
Used to Be • Phineas L. MacGuire . . . Blasts Off! • Phineas L.
MacGuire . . . Erupts! • Phineas L. MacGuire . . . Gets Slimed!
The Second Life of Abigail Walker • The Secret Language of Girls
Shooting the Moon • The Sound of Your Voice, Only Really Far
Away • Ten Miles Past Normal • Where I'd Like to Be*

$\mathbb{A}$
atheneum

ATHENEUM BOOKS FOR YOUNG READERS • An imprint of Simon & Schuster
Children's Publishing Division • 1230 Avenue of the Americas, New York, New
York 10020 • This book is a work of fiction. Any references to historical events,
real people, or real places are used fictitiously. Other names, characters, places,
and events are products of the author's imagination, and any resemblance to
actual events or places or persons, living or dead, is entirely coincidental. • Text
copyright © 2014 by Frances O'Roark Dowell • Illustrations copyright © 2014 by
Preston McDaniels • All rights reserved, including the right of reproduction
in whole or in part in any form. • ATHENEUM BOOKS FOR YOUNG READERS is a
registered trademark of Simon & Schuster, Inc. • Atheneum logo is a trademark
of Simon & Schuster, Inc. • For information about special discounts for bulk
purchases, please contact Simon & Schuster Special Sales at 1-866-506-1949 or
business@simonandschuster.com. • The Simon & Schuster Speakers Bureau can
bring authors to your live event. For more information or to book an event, contact
the Simon & Schuster Speakers Bureau at 1-866-248-3049 or visit our website at
www.simonspeakers.com. • Book design by Sonia Chaghatzbanian • The text for
this book is set in Garth Graphic. • The illustrations for this book are rendered in
pencil. • Manufactured in the United States of America • 0913 OFF • First Edition •
10 9 8 7 6 5 4 3 2 1 • CIP data for this book is available from the Library of Congress •
ISBN 978-1-4814-1463-0 • ISBN 978-1-4814-0101-2 (eBook)

PHINEAS L. MACGUIRE . . .

GETS COOKING!

PART THREE: A RECIPE FOR DISASTER!

by FRANCES O'ROARK DOWELL

illustrated by PRESTON McDANIELS

Atheneum Books for Young Readers
New York London Toronto Sydney New Delhi

Phineas invited the school bully, Evan Forbes, over to dinner, hoping that homemade biscuits would change his mind about clobbering Phineas if he stops baking him a daily batch of brownies. Maybe it will even help Phineas figure out why Evan is a bully in the first place. All this brownie baking is getting exhausting, and Phineas really needs this plan to work or else he'll be stuck baking for Evan for the rest of his life. Besides, there's a $10,000 bake-off prize to focus on and Phineas doesn't have a recipe yet!

Evan Forbes ate eleven biscuits.

Eleven.

He smeared the first two with butter, and the next nine he just sort of inhaled straight from the basket.

It was actually pretty impressive.

"So, Evan, Mac tells us you boys are in the same class?" my mom asked in her polite hostess voice. She was buttering up her third biscuit.

Not that I was counting.

Evan shook his head. "Not the same class—just the same grade," he told her through a mouthful of crumbs. "I'm in Mr. Burch's class. He's a lot cooler than Mrs. Tuttle. She's got this weird thing about frogs."

"She's okay," I said. Actually, I think Mrs. Tuttle is awesome, but I thought it would be rude to argue with my guest.

Also, I didn't want to get clobbered.

It only took Evan about three minutes to eat. After he ate eleven biscuits, he chowed down the chicken in three bites and slurped up three servings of mashed potatoes in under sixty seconds.

He spent the rest of dinner making silly faces at Margaret to make her laugh.

And when dinner was over, he helped clear the table.

It was almost like he was an actual human being.

"You got an Xbox, Mac?" he asked when we were done taking the plates to the sink. "That's

how I like to wind down after dinner—playing a
few hours of video games."

"What about homework?" I asked.

Evan shrugged. "What about it? Some people
do it, I don't. Next subject."

"We don't actually have an Xbox," I told

him. "Or any gaming systems. My mom is sort of against them."

I waited for Evan to explode. Amazingly, he just shrugged again and said, "So what do you want to do? My nanny—er, assistant—isn't picking me up until seven thirty."

Here's the funny thing: Evan Forbes looked smaller in my house than he did at school. Maybe that's why I actually had the guts to ask him to help me with my survey.

"Let me get this straight," he said as he followed me up the stairs to my room. "You want me to help you come up with questions about bullies?"

"Not just about bullies," I told him. "But about kids who've been bullied."

He seemed to think about this for a second. "Yeah, I could help you. I mean, I got bullied a lot in second grade. Remember Jason Thedrow?"

"Sort of. But he doesn't go to our school anymore, does he?"

"Nah, he moved. But he was, like, totally all

over my case in first and second grade."

I had to use all my willpower not to turn around and stare at him. Evan Forbes used to get bullied?

Totally weird.

I opened the door to my room and waved Evan in. A person's reaction to my room is a big test for whether or not we can be friends. If you are the sort of person who likes rooms that are neat and tidy, with all the clothes put away and all the books in the bookshelves, we're probably not going to get along all that well. Because my room is the total opposite of that.

In other words, if you can deal with chaos, we'll get along just fine.

"Awesome!" Evan exclaimed as he looked around. "I wish I could have my room like this."

That's when I had a very strange thought. Question: Was it possible that Evan Forbes and I might become friends?

"I mean, like, I never knew that a dweeb like you could have such a cool bedroom."

Answer: Highly doubtful.

Evan walked around, admiring my mold museum, which is two shelves of mold samples I've been growing for a few months now, and checking out my collection of the Mysteries of Planet Zindar books.

"I have to keep my room totally neat," he told me. "Like, not one thing out of place. My dad does an inspection every night when he gets home from work, whether I'm still awake or not."

"What happens if your room doesn't pass inspection?"

"Then I have to clean it up immediately. Even if it's eleven at night and I'm asleep. My dad makes me wake up and make everything perfect."

I thought about my mom and dad and Lyle. None of them could care less whether or not my room is clean. Mostly all they care about is whether or not I'm happy and if I'm doing good at school.

All of a sudden, I felt totally lucky.

"So, anyway, you want to work on that survey?" I asked as Evan dive-bombed onto my bed. "I kind of need to get it done."

Evan sat up and shrugged. "Not really, but I guess I owe you for the biscuits, so, like, whatever."

I thought he owed me for a whole lot more than the biscuits, but I decided not to mention it.

We spent the next twenty minutes coming up with questions. We had two lists, questions for kids who had been bullied and questions for kids who had bullied other kids.

"Maybe we ought to have questions for kids who've had both things happen," I suggested. "Like, maybe one year you might have been really mean to somebody, and the next year somebody was really mean to you."

"I hope somebody's jumping all over Jason Thedrow at his new school," Evan said, nodding. "He totally deserves it."

I stared at him.

He totally didn't get it.

Here's the funny thing: All of a sudden I realized that my stomach didn't hurt. It hadn't hurt all night, even though Evan had been in my personal space the whole time.

I had to wonder, scientifically speaking, what was going on.

Scientifically speaking, I'm pretty sure what was happening was pretty simple.

I wasn't scared of Evan Forbes anymore.

There were a lot of good explanations for this. One, the odds that Evan Forbes was going to clobber me in my own home were pretty small.

Two, the odds that Evan Forbes was going to clobber me in my own home after eating eleven biscuits I'd made myself were even smaller.

So, we're talking minimal fear factor here.

But there was another thing. Eating dinner with Evan, showing him my room, learning a little bit about his family—well, he was actually seeming sort of human to me. Like a real person.

And sure, you can be afraid of a real person, but it's hard to be afraid of a real person who spent half of dinner stuffing his face with biscuits and the other half making funny faces at your little sister.

Thinking about how Evan made Margaret laugh, I came to a decision. Tomorrow, no brownies. No waiting by the Dumpsters, no stomachache, no nothing.

Tomorrow I'd pretend like me and Evan Forbes were friends.

I mean, at least we weren't enemies anymore, right? And scientifically speaking, there's one thing I know for sure about friends, and that's that friends don't clobber each other.

At least that's what I was counting on. I'd have to look it up in *The Big Book of Best Friend Rules.*

So that thing about me pretending to be Evan Forbes's friend so he wouldn't clobber me? Turns out I didn't have to pretend. He was waiting for me when I got off the bus at school this morning.

"Yo, Mac! Buddy!" he called when he saw me. "I had this great idea last night when I got home from your place. You and me can start a baking business! Brownies and biscuits, dude. We'll make a killing! And I'll help bake. I'll meet you at your house this afternoon, and we can get started."

"Well, uh, I'm sort of supposed to go over to Ben's house this afternoon," I told him as we walked into the building together. Evan held the front door open for me, which was totally weird. "We're doing this recipe contest, and we need to finalize our plans."

"Sounds great," Evan said. "What time should I be there?"

So that problem where Evan Forbes was my enemy? It was possible that my problem now was that he was my friend.

"Evan Forbes is coming over to my apartment this afternoon?" Ben asked when I told him at lunch. "Since when did Evan Forbes start hanging around with people like you and me?"

I told him about asking Evan to come to dinner the night before. Aretha, who was sitting at her usual spot one table over, leaned toward us and said, "Brilliant plan, Mac! You ought to get the Nobel Peace Prize for that one."

"Yeah, but now he wants to go into business with me."

Aretha thought about this for a minute. "Just tell him you're a scientist and you don't have time to start a business."

"Yeah," Ben said. "Tell him you could help him get started, though. I'll do the PR."

I stared at him. "PR?"

"Yeah, you know—public relations. Publicity, advertising." Ben chomped on a pretzel stick. "If this recipe contest thing doesn't pan out, I might need a new line of work."

"So how is the recipe contest coming along?" Aretha asked.

"Oh, man! I can't believe I haven't told you guys this!" Ben's face lit up. "I've got the best recipe idea ever: salted pizza brownies with bacon."

I stared at Ben over my tuna fish sandwich. "Salted brownies?"

Ben nodded. "I've been reading all this stuff about food trends online? And salt is big. I

14

mean, it's huge, and when it comes to chocolate, it's humongous."

"But won't the bacon add salt to the brownies?"
I asked. Not that I was committed to the idea
of putting bacon into a perfectly good pizza
brownies recipe. But I like to be logical.

"The more salt the better, that's my motto!"
Ben exclaimed. "The thing is, last night I tried
out the pizza brownie recipe the way we talked
about—I used marshmallow fluff on top, which
worked great, and sprinkled it with
extra M&M's just like Mrs.
Klausenheimer said.
And it was good,
but it lacked a
special something.
So I made another
batch, but this
time I added an
extra teaspoon
of salt and half a
cup of crumbled

15

bacon. What can I say, Mac? They were genius brownies."

"Too much salt's bad for your heart."

Evan Forbes sat down in the seat next to me and opened up his lunchbox. "It's bad because it elevates your blood pressure. At least that's what my nanny—er, my assistant—says."

"But a little extra salt every once in a while is okay," Ben argued. At the same time he was looking at me like, *Really? Now we have to have lunch with him?* "You only eat one brownie at a time, right?"

"Not if you're me," Evan told him, taking a huge bite of a turkey sub. "I eat 'em by the dozens. But hey, me and Mac will give your brownies a try this afternoon, and if we like 'em, then we can definitely move forward with the recipe."

You know that cartoon thing where steam comes out of somebody's ears?

That's how you should imagine Ben looking right at that very second.

I glanced over at Aretha. You could tell she was finding this all very interesting. "You guys mind if I tag along this afternoon? I might be able to get something out of it for my food badge." She turned to Evan. "I'm a Girl Scout."

"That's cool," Evan said. "Sure, you can come." Then he crushed his milk carton and threw it at Mason Cutwelder's head. Mason yelled when the carton hit him, and Evan called out, "Sorry, dude! I was aiming for the trash can."

Only the trash can was in the opposite direction.

"Okay, I gotta go play some ball," Evan said, standing up. "You wanna play, Mac?"

I shook my head. "I, uh, have some homework I need to do."

"That's cool. I'll meet you on the bus after school."

Me, Ben, and Aretha all watched Evan walk out of the cafeteria. Then Ben turned to me and said, "You have got a serious problem on your hands, Mac. I don't know what's worse—having him for an enemy or having him for a friend."

Instead of going out to the playground for recess, I went to the library with my notebook. I needed to do some serious thinking.

First, I made a list called Good Things Right Now. That list included stuff like:

1. I am no longer worried about Evan Forbes clobbering me.
2. I know how to make the following

Good things about Evan Forbes
1. I am no longer worried about Evan Forbes clobbering me.
Bad things about Evan Forbes
1. Evan Forbes is my friend.
2. Evan Forbes wants to start a business with me.
3. Evan Forbes wants to take over my life.

things for dinner: chicken and mashed potatoes, spaghetti, waffles, biscuits, and Cheerios with milk.

3. I make the best brownies of any fourth-grade scientist in the United States, maybe the world.

4. I have about a hundred ideas for next year's science fair, including experiments with yeast, baking powder, baking soda, lemon juice, colloids, and emulsions.

The Bad Things list looked like this:

1. Evan Forbes is my friend.
2. Evan Forbes wants to start a business with me.
3. Evan Forbes wants to take over my life.
4. I still haven't figured out how to make brownies explode.

The good things on my Good Things list were definitely really good.

But the bad things on my Bad Things list?

I was pretty sure the first three were going to ruin my life.

Riding the bus home this afternoon, I started reading through some of the bullying questionnaires that kids had filled out. I'd passed the questions around this morning, and by lunchtime twenty people had answered them and turned in their papers.

It turns out kids have a lot to say about kids being mean to other kids. To me, the most interesting facts were:

1. Everybody answered "yes" to the question, "Has another kid ever been mean to you (called you names, hit or pushed you, threatened you)?"
2. Twelve of the twenty responders answered "yes" to the question, "Have you ever been mean to another kid?"
3. When asked why they'd been mean to another kid, every single person answered, "I don't know."

I thought about the reasons Ben had given me for being mean to Chester Oliphant. The funny thing is, none of them really had anything to do with Chester. They all had to do with Ben. It wasn't like he had anything personal against Chester.

He just had something personal against himself.

I took a quick look at Evan, who was sitting next to me. He was busy poking the kid in the seat in front of us with a ballpoint pen. The kid was totally ignoring him, which just made Evan poke him harder.

I thought about how I never stood up for myself when Evan was being mean to me. Now I sort of wish I had, even if it meant getting clobbered.

"Quit it," I told Evan now. "That kid didn't do anything to you."

Evan looked at me. "The back of his head is bugging me."

"Well, it's bugging me that you keep poking him. Leave him alone."

"Okay," Evan said, shrugging. "Whatever."

Evan started tapping the bus window with his pen, and the kid who'd been getting poked turned around and gave me a quick smile.

Maybe instead of a Labrador whisperer, I should be a bully whisperer.

When Evan and I got to Ben's apartment, Aretha was already there. So was Mrs. Klausenheimer.

And so was Killer.

As soon as he saw Killer, Evan pulled me back out into the hallway. "You didn't say anything about dogs. I can't be in the same room as a dog."

"Are you allergic?"

"No, not exactly. It's just—well, me and dogs don't mix. I don't like them, and they don't like me."

In other words, Evan Forbes was scared.

"Listen," I told him. "Killer's actually a really

nice dog. He looks like he'd tear your head off if he got a chance, but he's not like that at all."

"That dog? Nice? I don't think so!"

Now it's true that Killer is a humongous German shepherd with the biggest teeth you've ever seen. And it's true he looks like the sort of dog that would eat you for lunch. But inside

all that fur and those razorlike incisors beats a canine heart of gold.

"You don't have to be afraid of Killer, I promise," I told Evan. "All it takes is a treat, and he'll be your friend for life."

"I'm not afraid." Evan's face was totally red. "I just don't like dogs."

"If you're not afraid, then come back inside and I'll show you how nice Killer is. We can do a kind of experiment. That is, if you're really not afraid."

Evan didn't have a choice. He followed me back into Ben's apartment.

I went into the kitchen and got a couple of pieces of cooked bacon from Ben's bacon collection in the fridge. Ben liked to have at least half a pound of fried bacon ready at any time, in case he got any new bacon recipe inspirations. Tearing a piece in half, I called, "Come here, Killer!" Killer came galloping over to where I stood, practically knocking me over.

"Here's a treat, boy!" I told him, and held

out a piece of bacon. He slurped it out of my hand, and when he was done gulping it down, he licked me all over my face.

Did I mention that Killer is a very slobbery dog?

Then I handed the other piece of bacon to Evan. "If you give this to Killer, he'll be your friend for life."

"Maybe I don't want a friend for life."

I gave Evan a hard look. "I thought you said you weren't afraid."

Evan sighed. "I'm not. Give me the stupid bacon."

His hand was shaking. "Here, Killer," he whispered in a squeaky voice.

Killer snatched the bacon from him, gulped it down, and then covered Evan Forbes with kisses. He knocked Evan down and licked him all over his face and hands.

At first Evan was doing this squeaky scream thing, and Mrs. Klausenheimer looked worried, like maybe we should pull Killer off him. But

then all of a sudden, Evan started laughing.

"You're slobbering on me, you stupid dog!"

And that was all it took.

Evan Forbes and Killer had bonded.

For the rest of the afternoon, while Ben, Aretha, and I made brownies, Evan played with Killer in the living room while Mrs. Klausenheimer watched from the couch. When it was time to go home, she smiled at him and said, "If I had a grandson, I'd want him to be just like you, Evan. You're so good with Killer. If you were my grandson, you could come over every afternoon and play with him. I can't give him all the exercise he needs."

Evan was quiet for a minute. Then he said, "I could come over in the afternoons and play with Killer. I could sort of pretend I was your grandson. I never see my real grandparents, anyway."

Mrs. Klausenheimer bounced on the couch with excitement. "Oh, that would be lovely! I'll bake you cookies every day! Do you like oatmeal raisin?"

Riding the elevator down to the ground floor, Evan said, "I guess I can't go into the baking business with you, Mac, now that me and Killer are going to be hanging out every day."

"That's okay," I told him. "I'm getting a little sick of brownies."

"Those pizza ones are pretty good, though," Evan said. "Except I don't think you should use real pepperoni."

"That was Ben's idea. He likes to experiment."

Evan nodded. "I can tell. Who knew a bacon milk shake would taste so good, though, right?"

"You learn something new every day," I agreed.

The phone rang while I was scrambling eggs. Scrambled eggs is now my go-to meal on days when I have lots of homework or have spent most of the afternoon hanging out with Ben or walking Lemon Drop.

Here's the trick to great scrambled eggs: Keep the heat low and cook 'em slow.

That's all there is to it.

"Mac, phone's for you," Sarah called from the living room, where she and Margaret were having a fashion show. "It's a girl!"

The way she said, "It's a girl" was all sing-songy and romantic.

I pretty much broke out in hives just from the sound of her voice.

"It's Aretha, so quit breaking out in hives," Aretha said when I grabbed the phone from Sarah. "I'm calling because I need help."

I turned the heat way down under the eggs. "All right, but I can't talk for long. I'm putting dinner on the table."

Okay, that sounded sort of weird.

"I need to figure out how to make exploding brownies," Aretha said. "Or some kind of crazy food. It's for the food science part of this badge I'm working on. I could do something boring like a presentation on lemon juice, but I want drama. I almost fell asleep at our last meeting, the presentations were so boring."

"So you want dramatic food?"

"That's right, Mac. I want food that will make everybody spin in their seats. Can you help me?"

"Meet me at the playground at recess tomorrow," I told her. "I'll have a report."

As I spooned the eggs onto the plates, I had a strange feeling. It was like I was remembering something I used to know but had sort of forgotten.

Like, oh yeah, I'm a scientist.

If I'd been wearing an apron, I would have flung it off. It wasn't that I was tired of cooking. I sort of liked cooking. But every night?

Not so much.

At dinner, I looked around the table and said, "I have an announcement. From now on, I'll cook dinner two nights a week. If we have pizza and Cheerios® all the other nights, that's fine with me. I am a scientist, and I have work to do. Cooking is a full-time job."

My mom thought about this. "It's true, cooking has been taking up a lot of your time. And your scientific work is important."

"Maybe I could make some freezer meals on the weekends," Lyle said. "There was an article

34

in the paper the other day about a woman who does all her cooking for the month on one day—stews, casseroles, you name it. Then she puts everything in the freezer, and every morning she takes something out to thaw."

"You'd need a pretty big freezer to pull that off," I pointed out.

"Ours is big enough for a couple of casseroles at least," Lyle said. "If your mom makes dinner Sunday nights, then we're set."

"Great," I said, pushing my chair away from the table. "Now I need to go make some food explode."

When you're a genius fourth-grade scientist, you keep files about all sorts of scientific matters. I keep my files in a shoe box in my closet, next to the shoe boxes filled with my dried earthworm collection and the shoe boxes with my dried fungus collection.

I have a very interesting closet. Though it does smell sort of funny.

I pulled out my scientific files shoe box and

dumped its contents on my bed. There was stuff I'd clipped out of the newspaper and from magazines, like articles about Pluto losing its planet status (totally unfair, in my opinion), and notes I'd taken when I was coming up with ideas for my mold museum (my favorite idea was having the museum in the bathroom, because mold likes humid places, but my mom said no way). There were ads for chemistry sets I wasn't going to be allowed to get until I was fifty, but I still liked to dream about.

And then there were my notebooks. I like to get those really little spiral notebooks that you can put in your back pocket. That way, if I get a scientific genius idea or come across some scientifically super-important information, I can write it down right away.

I started flipping through the articles and my notebooks to see if I could find anything about exploding food. I found something about exploding soda cans, and how to make an exploding cake using dry ice, which sounded way too awesome and too dangerous for any adult to give it the thumbs-up.

Okay, I said to myself, lying back against my pillow, what are we trying to accomplish here? Aretha wants drama and excitement, but the fact is, she's really trying to demonstrate something about food science. So what do I know about food science from personal experience?

I knew about emulsions and colloids. I knew how to curdle milk. I knew that if you didn't put enough baking powder in your waffle batter, your waffles would fall flat. But.

But!

What if you put in too much?

"So you're saying I should make exploding waffles?" Aretha asked me the next day at recess. We were sitting on the swings, with one empty swing between us so that no one would think we were swinging together.

I nodded, and Aretha smiled. "I like it," she said. "I like it a lot. It's about time someone did

something to stir my troop up, and this ought to do the trick."

Just then Ben showed up. When Aretha told him about the exploding waffle idea, he got this big grin on his face. "I have a stupendazoid idea. You ought to add food coloring. Imagine it—exploding green waffles. I could film it and put it on YouTube. We'd be famous!"

"Green is the color of the Girl Scout uniform," Aretha said. "Plus, it might add a little more pizzazz to the whole project. Let's do it!"

At lunch, we went to the library to find a good waffle recipe on the Internet. As it turns out, there are over two million waffle recipes on the Internet, so we just checked out the first five and picked the simplest one. Then we did some research on baking powder so that Aretha understood the science behind the waffle explosion.

"So baking powder is made by combining baking soda with an acid," Aretha said, taking notes as she talked. "When you add a liquid like water or milk, the acid and the base interact, and that creates carbon dioxide, which makes the stuff fizz up."

She looked up from her notes. "Basically, if our experiment works, the baking powder will produce a whole lot of carbon dioxide."

"Which is a kind of gas," Ben added.

"Which will make the waffles explode instead of just rise while they're baking," I finished up. "At least, that's our hypothesis."

Aretha grinned. "I'm glad we're doing this at Ben's house and not mine."

Ben was the only one of us with a waffle iron and a mom who wouldn't go nuts over somebody exploding waffles in her kitchen.

"So do you think we could explode brownies by putting in too much baking powder?" Ben asked as we walked back to Mrs. Tuttle's class. "Because our recipe's due pretty soon, and I'm not feeling all that confident about it."

"One, I don't think exploding brownies will taste all that good," I told him. "And two, the problem with your recipe is the pepperoni. Bacon is fine, but pepperoni is going too far."

Ben thought about this for a minute. "You could be right. Maybe I should take out the pepperoni and add some beef jerky."

"Have you ever thought about just making plain brownies?" Aretha asked. "Maybe with chocolate frosting to jazz them up a little bit?"

Ben and I looked at each other. Plain brownies with chocolate frosting?

"No way," Ben said.

"I don't think so," I said.

"No offense or anything," Ben told Aretha, "but really? I'm trying to win a recipe contest and that's what you come up with?"

Aretha shrugged. "Simple is good. Simple works."

"Simple's boring," I told her. "We need brownies that make a statement. We need life-altering brownies, brownies that pop—" I glanced at Ben, looking for a little backup here, but it was

41

clear that at the moment he was too busy thinking to talk.

Which is always a dangerous thing.

"Simple," Ben muttered. "Simple and to the
point. That's boring, all right, but you know
what would make it a lot less boring?"

"If you sprinkled bacon on top?" I guessed.

"Exacto-mundo!" Ben exclaimed, back at full
volume. "Bacon and chocolate
chips! That turns

a simple, boring recipe into a classic recipe!" He pounded me on the back. "Mac, you're a genius!"

Aretha and I watched as Ben skipped down the hallway.

"Well, at least you got him to take the pepperoni out," Aretha said.

"At least the brownies won't explode all over the judges," I said.

Aretha and I slapped high fives.

Scientifically speaking, it had been a good day.

Here are some helpful hints when
it comes to making exploding green waffles:

1. Spread newspapers over the kitchen
counters and the floor. Like, three
days' worth of newspapers. And I
mean, put them everywhere. You
will be amazed by how far exploding
waffle batter can travel.

2. If you get green food coloring on your

hands, you will have green hands for at least three days, even if you wash them a hundred times. Believe me, I know.

3. The best thing about exploding waffles is watching them explode.

4. After your waffles explode, you will not be tempted to eat them.

5. Your supervising adult should be the sort of person who's very relaxed and easygoing. It might also be good if they're taking a nap while you're making the waffles.

Fortunately, our supervising adult was Mrs. Klausenheimer. After she showed us how to use the waffle iron and warned us approximately six million times not to burn ourselves, she took her usual place on the couch and pulled a copy of *Celebrity Dogs and Race Cars* from her purse. She yelled, "You kids be careful in there!" every few minutes, but other than that, she pretty much left us alone.

Waffles, in case you're wondering, are really easy to make. Actually, one thing I've learned from all this cooking stuff? Almost everything is really easy to make. You just have to have good directions, and you have to follow them. I mean, okay, baked Alaska probably isn't easy, but other stuff? You'd be surprised.

Anyway, waffle batter is pretty basic: Flour, eggs, milk, salt, vegetable oil, and baking powder. Exploding green waffle batter is pretty much the same, only add a bunch of green food coloring and triple the baking powder.

And then stand back.

"All right, folks, this is the big moment, what we've all been waiting for," Ben said as he circled me and Aretha with his video camera, and then pulled in for a close-up of the waffle maker. "Mac and Aretha have carefully mixed together the ingredients for the world's most delicious— and most explosive—waffles. Now watch closely as Aretha carefully pours the batter onto the hot waffle iron. . . . Yes! The batter is on the iron!

Aretha slowly pulls down the lid . . . now wait for it . . . wait for it . . ."

We waited. And waited. And kept waiting.

Ben checked his watch. "Should it be taking this long?"

"I don't know," Aretha said. "I've never tried exploding waffles before."

Just when I thought nothing was going to happen, three things happened at the same time:

1. Killer burst through the front door, pulling Evan Forbes along with him.
2. Mrs. Klausenheimer snored the loudest snore ever recorded in human history. In fact, it was so loud that Killer started barking like crazy, Evan yelled like somebody had tackled him from behind, and Ben jumped a mile high and dropped his camera.
3. Which is too bad, because approximately two seconds later, the waffles exploded.

You know that thing I said before about putting newspapers on the counters and the floor?

Well, we didn't actually do that.

Which was too bad, because exploding waffles make a humongous mess.

Maybe you're imagining waffles exploding sort of being like popcorn popping. That's the wrong thing to imagine. First of all, exploding waffles don't wait until they're fully baked to explode. Exploding waffles are half-baked waffles. Another word for half-baked waffles is lava waffles. Okay, "lava waffles" is two words, but you get my point. Visualize lava pouring out of a volcano. It flows like a river. It flows over everything. It covers the floor.

That's your exploding waffle in a nutshell.

Here's something interesting I learned today: German shepherds love exploding green waffles. How did I learn this?

Guess.

When we saw what a mess the exploding waffles were making, everybody started yelling, "Get the paper towels!" and "Get a mop!" What we should have been yelling was "Get Killer!"

As soon as he sniffed that something was up, Killer was in the kitchen. From the look in his eyes, you would have sworn he'd spent all his life dreaming of the day he'd find a kitchen filled with green, half-baked waffle batter. You could practically see him licking his lips.

And then he was licking waffle batter. He licked it off the floor and then he stood up on his hind legs and was licking it off the counters. By this time, Ben had picked up his camera, so of course he was filming. "This is definitely going on YouTube!" he kept yelling. "It's gonna go viral!"

Evan stood in the kitchen doorway and said, "If this is what's for dinner, I'm going to McDonald's."

Aretha was grinning from ear to ear. "The Girl Scouts will never forget this. I'm going to be a legend."

"Maybe you should only double the baking powder when you do this for your troop," I suggested.

"Are you kidding? I'm going to quadruple it! I'm going to make waffles that fly out of the windows."

After Killer had filled up on exploded green waffles, everybody cleaned up what was left, even Evan.

I think Killer was having a good influence on him.

Sarah Fortemeyer came at five to give me and Aretha a ride home. After she dropped off Aretha, Sarah looked at me and asked, "Are you feeling okay?"

"I feel great," I told her. "We just did an amazing experiment. The cool thing is, I came up with a hypothesis—that tripling the amount of baking powder in the waffle batter would make the waffles explode—and I was totally right. That's a really big deal for a scientist."

"That's great, Mac," Sarah said. "Only, you're looking a little green."

I looked green for the next three days.

Nobody teased me, though.

Evan Forbes wouldn't let them.

It's been weird having Evan Forbes for a friend, but it's not all bad. First of all, Ben and I are training him not to throw his milk cartons at people's heads at lunch, so we're practically the most popular kids in the fourth grade. Secondly, if you need someone to test out brownie recipes on, Evan is definitely your man. He can eat two dozen without even blinking. Or burping, which is even more impressive.

The day before the recipe contest deadline, me, Ben, Aretha, and Evan had a vote. It was between pizza brownies made with maraschino cherries, marshmallows and M&M's, and frosted brownies sprinkled with bacon and chocolate chips.

The bacon and chocolate chips won hands down.

Unfortunately, our recipe didn't.

Ben was bummed, but he got over it. For one thing, his exploding waffles video has gotten

forty-nine hits on YouTube, which is forty-eight more than his last video did. For another thing, he's gained five pounds from eating brownies.

In Ben's opinion, genius artists should be on the chubby side.

Speaking of five pounds, my mom has lost five pounds since I started cooking. I guess I could take that as an insult, except she eats everything I put in front of her. Now that we only have pizza once a week, she eats a lot more baked chicken and salad.

Okay, and the occasional bowl of Cheerios.

Hey, I'm a scientist. I can't be cooking up huge feasts all the time.

I've got work to do. ∿

FRANCES O'ROARK DOWELL is the bestselling and critically acclaimed author of *Dovey Coe*, *The Second Life of Abigail Walker*, *Chicken Boy*, *Falling In*, *Where I'd Like to Be*, *The Secret Language of Girls*, and of course, the Phineas L. MacGuire series. She lives with her husband and two sons in Durham, North Carolina.

Connect with Frances online at FrancesDowell.com.